Mouse moves house

Russell Punter

Adapted from a story by Phil Roxbee Cox

Illustrated by Stephen Cartwright

Designed by Hope Reynolds
Edited by Jenny Tyler and Lesley Sims
Reading consultants: Alison Kelly and Anne Washtell

There is a little yellow duck to find on every page.

"Goodbye old hole. I'm off!"
cries Mouse.

Today's the day that she moves house.

She helps her dad to
pack the plates.

"Well done," says Dad.
"I'll stack the crates."

A box of socks is hard to pack.

"I'll pop Dad's vase in this black sack."

Mouse takes the paintings off the wall.

Now they can go.
Dad rolls the rug.

Dad helps Mouse out
with her blue pack.

When Mouse runs out,
Dad shouts...

Come back!

"A big black cat!" Dad gives a yelp.

"Dad, this is Fat Cat,
come to help!"

Cat guides the mice
to their new house.

"Home sweet home, at last,"
sighs Mouse.

Thanks,
Fat Cat!

Puzzles

Puzzle 1

Can you find the
words that rhyme?

Mouse   stack
pack   hole
box   house
roll   snug
rug   socks

Puzzle 2

One word is wrong in this speech bubble.
What should it say?

Puzzle 3
Can you find these things in the picture?

Mouse   crate

pan   spoon

cups   stool

Puzzle 4
Choose the right speech bubble for the picture.

Answers to puzzles

Puzzle 1

Mouse ⟶ house

pack ⟶ stack

box ⟶ socks

roll ⟶ hole

rug ⟶ snug

Puzzle 2

Don't make them <u>fall!</u>

Puzzle 3

Mouse

crate

cups

pan

spoon

stool

Puzzle 4

About phonics

Phonics is a method of teaching reading used extensively in today's schools. At its heart is an emphasis on identifying the *sounds* of letters, or combinations of letters, that are then put together to make words. These sounds are known as phonemes.

Starting to read

Learning to read is an important milestone for any child. The process can begin well before children start to learn letters and put them together to read words. The sooner children can discover books and enjoy stories and language, the better they will be prepared for reading themselves, first with the help of an adult and then independently.

You can find out more about phonics on the Usborne Very First Reading website, **Usborne.com/veryfirstreading** (US readers go to **www.veryfirstreading.com**). Click on the **Parents** tab at the top of the page, then scroll down and click on **About synthetic phonics**.

Phonemic awareness

An important early stage in pre-reading and early reading is developing phonemic awareness: that is, listening out for the sounds within words. Rhymes, rhyming stories and alliteration are excellent ways of encouraging phonemic awareness.

In this story, your child will soon identify the *ou* sound, as in **mouse** and **house**. Look out, too, for rhymes such as **roll** – **hole** and **black** – **sack**.

Hearing your child read

If your child is reading a story to you, don't rush to correct mistakes, but be ready to prompt or guide if he or she is struggling. Above all, give plenty of praise and encouragement.

This edition first published in 2020 by Usborne Publishing Ltd., Usborne House, 83-85 Saffron Hill, London EC1N 8RT, England. usborne.com Copyright © 2020, 2006, 2002 Usborne Publishing Ltd.